KIDS C
THE CHOOSE
OWN ADVENTURE® STORIES!

"Choose Your Own Adventure is the best thing that has come along since books themselves."
—Alysha Beyer, age 11

"I didn't read much before, but now I read my Choose Your Own Adventure books almost every night."
—Chris Brogan, age 13

"I love the control I have over what happens next."
—Kosta Efstathiou, age 17

"Choose Your Own Adventure books are so much fun to read and collect—I want them all!"
—Brendan Davin, age 11

And teachers like this series, too:

"We have read and reread, worn thin, loved, loaned, bought for others, and donated to school libraries our Choose Your Own Adventure books."

CHOOSE YOUR OWN ADVENTURE®— AND MAKE READING MORE FUN!

HOSTAGE!

BY EDWARD PACKARD

ILLUSTRATED BY RON WING

BANTAM BOOKS
NEW YORK • TORONTO • LONDON • SYDNEY • AUCKLAND

RL4, age 10 and up

HOSTAGE!
A Bantam Book / February 1996

*CHOOSE YOUR OWN ADVENTURE® is a registered
trademark of Bantam Books,
a division of Bantam Doubleday Dell Publishing Group, Inc.
Registered in the U.S. Patent and Trademark Office and
elsewhere.*

Original conception of Edward Packard

*Cover art by Jeff Mangiat
Interior illustrations by Ron Wing*

*All rights reserved.
Copyright © 1996 by Edward Packard.
Cover art and illustrations copyright © 1996 by
Bantam Books.
No part of this book may be reproduced or transmitted in any
form or by any means, electronic or mechanical, including
photocopying, recording, or by any information storage and
retrieval system, without permission in writing from
the publisher.
For information address: Bantam Books.*

*If you purchased this book without a cover you should be aware
that this book is stolen property. It was reported as "unsold and
destroyed" to the publisher and neither the author nor the publisher has received any payment for this "stripped book."*

ISBN 0-553-56627-X

Published simultaneously in the United States and Canada

Bantam Books are published by Bantam Books, a division of
Bantam Doubleday Dell Publishing Group, Inc. Its trademark,
consisting of the words "Bantam Books" and the portrayal of a
rooster, is Registered in the U.S. Patent and Trademark Office and
in other countries. Marca Registrada. Bantam Books, 1540
Broadway, New York, New York 10036.

PRINTED IN THE UNITED STATES OF AMERICA

OPM   0 9 8 7 6 5 4 3 2 1

HOSTAGE!

WARNING!!!

Do not read this book straight through from beginning to end. These pages contain many dif-
ferent adventures you may have when you and
your classmates are taken hostage by an infa-
mous drug cartel in the heart of our nation's
capital.

From time to time as you read along, you will be
asked to make a choice. You are responsible for
the adventures you have because you choose.
After you make a decision, follow the directions
to find out what happens to you next.

Think carefully before you act. The people holding you hostage are hardened international
criminals who will stop at nothing to get what
they want. You will have to move quickly and de-
cisively. Your choices may make you a hero, or
they may put the entire nation in danger.

Good luck!

Your class from school is on a field trip, touring Washington, D.C., for the weekend. You have already visited the Air and Space Museum, the Capitol, the Supreme Court, and the Vietnam Veterans Memorial. Right now you're on a bus headed for the White House. Your group is getting a special tour. The president is away on a trip, and Ms. Sealy, your teacher, has promised you'll get a peek at the Oval Office.

You reach Pennsylvania Avenue and glimpse the White House through the trees. To your surprise, the way ahead is blocked. Police are rerouting traffic. Ms. Sealy is standing in the aisle of the bus, talking on a cellular phone. She's a tall, slim woman and wears her hair in bangs. She used to be a tennis champion. She's a champion teacher, too. That's why it was your class that got to take this trip.

Everyone is talking. Liam Neilson, sitting behind you, is carrying on the loudest, as usual.

"Why didn't we take a helicopter?" he cries.

"Why didn't we go to Disneyland?" another kid yells.

"Get us out of here!" someone chimes in.

They quiet down as the bus lurches and the driver suddenly turns onto a side street, away from the White House.

Ms. Sealy clicks off her phone and calls for attention.

Turn to page 2.

"Sorry, kids, all White House tours have been canceled. They've tightened security because of the threat of a terrorist attack by the Alarin cartel. We're going to visit the National Cathedral instead—it's just a few blocks from our hotel, so we can walk back there afterward."

A chorus of groans goes up. Liam yells, "Can't we do something interesting?"

Some of these kids are really stupid. They think that how they're going to spend the afternoon is more important than whether there's a terrorist attack. And the Alarin cartel is no joke. It's the biggest international crime syndicate the world has ever known. The cartel leaders own a couple of islands in the Caribbean and another in the South Pacific, and they have hidden bases all over the world. From their remote camps in South America they direct drug and arms traffic and prey on legitimate businesses, taking in billions of dollars each month. The United States and other countries are trying to break their grip. The president has said that the cartel is at war with civilized society and that it may be necessary to invade their island bases to stop them.

The bus turns onto Wisconsin Avenue. Ms. Sealy is still standing in the aisle, talking about the cathedral. "It's one of the largest in the world. When you go through it, you'll see a stained-glass window with a moon rock embedded in it . . ." She stops. The bus has halted. Cops are holding up traffic.

Go on to the next page.

"I don't know what this is all about," Ms. Sealy says. "But our hotel is only three blocks from here. We can walk if we have to." She lurches as the bus driver starts up, turns sharply, and heads down a side street to avoid the wait. Unfortunately the street he has turned onto is blocked off at the other end.

Ms. Sealy leans down and exchanges a few words with the driver. Then she calls out, "He says he can let us out up ahead and we can walk from there."

Turn to page 4.

The bus moves partway down the street, but suddenly the driver hits the brakes as three men dressed in battle fatigues and flak jackets run out in front. They are armed with assault weapons. One of them breaks open the door of the bus and jumps aboard. He trains his weapon on the driver and begins yelling orders in a thick accent. The driver pulls the bus up onto the sidewalk and grinds ahead in low gear, knocking over a trash can. Then, obviously doing as he's told, he drives through an open gate and continues about fifty yards up a drive before pulling to a stop.

The drive leads to a rectangular concrete building, two stories high. The grounds around it are mixed woods, lawns, and shrubbery. Looking back, you watch a man dressed like the others shut the grilled iron doors of the entrance gate. He snaps on a chain, locks it, and walks back to the little guardhouse nearby.

The man on the bus gets off, yelling, "Stay put!" as he leaves.

Turn to page 6.

6

The bus is filled with noise and confusion. Some kids are yelling, some crying or whimpering. The driver turns and stares at his passengers. He looks as frightened as the rest.

Ms. Sealy holds up her hands and calls for attention. Gradually the kids quiet down. "Children, the best thing we can do now is keep quiet and calm. I know I can count on you."

Almost everyone calls out, "You can," or, "Yes, Ms. Sealy."

"Now, according to my map," she goes on, "we're on the grounds of the Biological Research Institute. They obviously want us as hostages, but I don't think we'll be harmed. We'd lose our value to them if we were."

Everyone starts talking at once except for a couple of kids who are wailing as if they were being led to the slaughterhouse. You comfort the girl sobbing beside you, which makes you feel calmer yourself.

Meanwhile, your mind is racing, wondering if there is any way to escape. You're in the aisle seat only two rows from the front of the bus. You have a pretty good view. The man who just got off the bus is standing on the grass a dozen yards or so away. He has an automatic weapon strapped on his shoulder. The two men you saw before aren't in sight. They may be in the guardhouse near the front gate.

Ann Stoddart, across the aisle from you, has a radio, which she's holding close to her ear.

You lean toward her. "Is this on the news?"

Turn to page 62.

A terrorist guard brings you up to the conference room. Marcos, surrounded by his advisers, is waiting. He looks angry even before you start talking.

You recite the president's message, hoping you have remembered every word. Marcos grows agitated. His face reddens as he listens.

When you finish, he leans toward you, trying to keep calm but barely controlling the anger in his voice. "What was the president's tone of voice when he said this? How did he look?"

"His tone was very firm. He looked very serious."

"Was he angry?" The question comes from a bearded man in the corner.

"I would say he was, but his voice was very steady. He was very cool."

Marcos leans back and folds his hands. His eyes never leave you. "Tell us once again what the president said."

"You've already taped it," you say, motioning to the recorder on the table.

"Tell us!"

Obviously they want to see if you'll change your story the second time, but you repeat what you said before word for word.

"All right, Champ," Marcos says. "Wait in the next room."

A guard leads you out and locks you in the office next door. You wait for the terrorists to decide your fate, and perhaps that of a great many others as well.

Turn to page 106.

You take off, keeping in as straight a line as you can. When you come back a couple of minutes later, the guard is standing in the doorway of the bus. He smiles at you.

"You be traffic cop," he says. "Anyone else wants to go, you let them, but one at a time, you understand? This is your job."

"Yeah, sure," you say.

"You let more than one go at a time, or they don't come back, and I shoot you." He whips his gun toward your face so fast you shrink back. He laughs. He's kidding, but maybe not completely.

He gestures behind him. "Go back and tell them. Stay near the door and make sure they follow the rules. You going to be the champ."

Champ? This jerk has an odd sense of humor, you think. But you go in and tell everyone his rules. The bus driver is the next to go. You hold up your hand, indicating that no one else can go until he comes back. You realize that in a way you're helping the terrorists do their job. On the other hand, you are making it easier for the others on the bus.

Turn to page 63.

"Halt!" the guard screams and starts after him. But then he remembers the vial lying on the floor where anyone could knock it over. He picks it up, gently cradling it in both hands, and sets it on the desk outside the Containment Room. Then he races after Dr. Kostrikis. He seems to have forgotten completely about you!

For a minute or so the vial will be unguarded. You could just take it. But they're bound to hunt you down if you do.

Suddenly you get an idea. You remember glancing at one of the vials in the storeroom that looked a lot like this one: the same shape and about three inches high. You don't know what's in the other one, but at least it's not the EF1 virus. You could take it and substitute it for the real vial. Then they would never know that the real EF1 vial was missing.

Or would they? The vial you're thinking of had a slight purplish hue, unlike the clear one on the guard's desk. Still, it seems worth a try.

You rush back to the storeroom, get the other vial, and then hurry toward the desk. You're about ten feet from it when a couple of terrorists appear from around the corner.

"Freeze!"

You hold up your hands, the harmless vial clutched in one of them.

They keep their guns trained on you. The closest one walks slowly toward you.

Turn to page 40.

"What's happening?" you ask. "With the terrorists?"

"I don't know much," says Dr. Kostrikis. "They've obviously seized control of this building. There's not much question why. There is a virus kept here known as the EF1. It's tremendously dangerous, but we've been studying it because there's a possibility it could open up a way to cure certain forms of cancer. The downside is that if it gets loose, it could be fatal to a large population in a matter of days. My colleagues and I have developed a counteragent—a medicine we think can overcome this virus. It's not been tested on humans, however. There's a danger the side effects might be just as bad as the disease. Meanwhile, of course, we've kept the EF1 tightly guarded."

"We heard about this on the bus," you say. "I guess that's the reason the army hasn't moved in."

"Exactly," Kostrikis says.

"What happened to the other people in the building?"

"Since it's the weekend, there were only a few others besides me," Kostrikis says. "I heard some firing—there must have been a brief shoot-out with the security guards. By now the others have probably either escaped or been captured. The terrorists searched, of course, but they missed me—I crawled into an air shaft, then moved into this storeroom."

Turn to page 102.

There are double doors on the front of the shed. Fortunately they're not locked. You swing one open and find a tractor, probably used for maintenance of the institute grounds. The key is in the ignition. You lurch over and haul yourself into the driver's seat, wondering if you could use it to escape. It's hard to believe you could get very far.

Still, making a try is better than cowering here until you're shot or bleed to death!

You turn the key. The tractor starts, and because it's already in gear, it leaps ahead with surprising speed, knocking the doors aside. You

step on the gas and take off toward the entrance gate. The driveway is barricaded by pickup trucks, parked cars, and the tour bus. You cut around to the side, steering through heavy brush. You hear dogs barking behind you, bullets whistling overhead.

You're only fifty yards from the gate. You can see army tanks and other vehicles stationed out on the street. Two terrorist guards with assault guns are standing by the guardhouse.

Turn to page 94.

14

You decide to wait for darkness. You feel pretty safe here, and it's better to put up with waiting, you reason, if it means a better chance of escape.

Huddled in the thicket, brushing off bugs and slapping at an occasional mosquito, you think about what's happening. The terrorists have threatened to let out the killer virus. And to back up their threat, they're holding a busload of kids imprisoned somewhere in the lab building. In a way you feel like a deserter. You hate being the only one who got away. But then you realize you haven't gotten away yet. You still have to get over that wall.

Night finally comes, except it doesn't really get dark. Floodlights set up on surrounding streets cast an eerie glow over the grounds of the institute. You're still afraid of being seen, but you don't have much choice. You've grown tremendously thirsty and hungry, hunched all these hours in the thicket. If you wait much longer, you'll be too weak to make it over the wall.

You peer out through the foliage. You see no sign of guards or dogs, but they may be hidden in the shadows, or behind some trees. You take a few deep breaths and dash out of the thicket, grab the log, and drag it toward the wall. It's heavier than you expected. You have to rest every few steps, then tug it along some more.

Turn to page 96.

"Mr. President," you say, "I just don't want to go back there."

His face falls. He purses his lips for a moment as if he's going to try to talk you into it. But then he shakes your hand. "That's all right," he says. "I had some misgivings about even suggesting it. My assistant, Ms. Stebbins here, will see that arrangements are made for your travel home. We'll ask you to stay in contact with us until the crisis is over. We might have some more questions at some point."

"Certainly, sir," you say. And you go along with the kindly looking woman who leads you out of the room.

An hour later, the special forces team storms the institute, rescues the hostages, and captures or kills every one of the terrorists. Unfortunately, the killer virus escapes, and the newly developed medicine that might have countered it is destroyed in the fighting.

You and your classmates are all safely back home by the time you get the news, but there's no cause for rejoicing. Forty thousand people have already died. The epidemic has spread far beyond Washington. Cases—and fatalities—have been reported in dozens of localities.

Turn to page 118.

You stop and raise your hands.

The guard comes up to you. He says something under his breath, then grips your wrist and spins you around.

"Hey!" you protest. You're certainly not a threat—he's almost twice your size, and he has a gun.

Instead of answering, he takes your arm and half-guides you, half-drags you down the side corridor and around a corner. He shoves you into an empty office. "Stay here or I'll have the dogs chew up your other leg!" he warns, and shuts the door in your face.

After that rough treatment your ankle begins hurting again, and more blood oozes out of your wound.

You turn off the glaring overhead light, leaving a desk lamp on so it's not completely dark. Then you lie down on the rug and try to sleep.

Sleep doesn't come. The pain in your ankle is getting worse. You let out a long, low moan. A moment later you hear a noise like a door opening.

"You must be a hostage," a voice says in clipped English. You half-turn and are astonished to see a man in a rumpled suit step out of a closet.

"*What* . . . who are you?" you murmur.

"Dr. Andrew Kostrikis. I'm a scientist with the institute," he says in a low voice. "I've been hiding in the closet." He glances anxiously at the door. "How did they get you?"

Turn to page 27.

You decide not to break the window. You might panic the terrorists and make them flee, but if you are contagious, you would risk spreading the virus. Millions might die, and it wouldn't save your life anyway.

You lie down on the bed and wait for what comes. You're a lot more tired than you realized, and you soon fall asleep. You awake about five A.M. feeling terribly weak and feverish. There's no doubt in your mind that you're a victim of the EF1 virus. During the hours ahead, you drift in and out of consciousness, getting steadily weaker, gradually losing all sense of time. Suddenly you're wakened by muffled explosions, gunfire, shouts. The government special forces have attacked!

Turn to page 28.

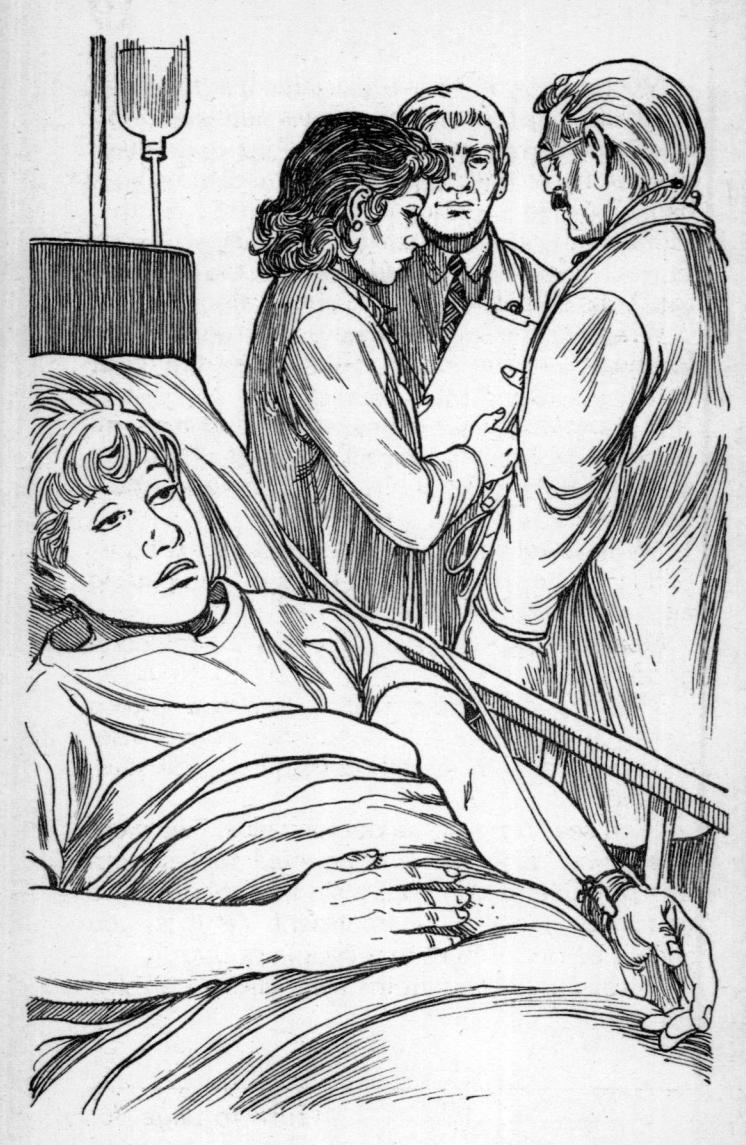

Much later you wake up again, this time in a bed with white sheets and pillows and with an IV attached to your arm. Through half-open eyes, you see two men and a woman standing by your bed. They're wearing white jackets. Stethoscopes dangle from their necks. They're talking to each other in hushed tones. One of them mentions something about an infection.

When you hear this, sweat breaks out on your forehead. You've been infected by the killer virus!

A woman in a nurse's uniform comes in. "Good news," she says to the others. "The test shows that the patient has only a bacterial infection."

"What a relief!" one of the doctors exclaims. Suddenly they're all smiling, chatting and patting each other on the back.

Hoarsely you whisper, "How is an infection good news?"

The woman in the nurse's uniform moves closer and presses her hand over yours. "Because we can cure it with antibiotics," she says, smiling.

"You see," one of the doctors adds, "we were afraid you might have contracted rabies from that dog bite. If you had, we'd have had to give you a nasty course of treatment. As it is, you should be out of here in a couple of days."

"I was afraid I caught the killer virus," you say.

Turn to page 86.

"There's no question about it. You have a full-blown case of the killer virus," he says. "But Dr. Kostrikis and his colleagues here at the institute have developed a new drug that may be able to cure it. We'd been planning to test it on rats beginning next week. But you can't wait that long. I just gave you a dose. It may cause terrible side effects, but it's your only chance of survival."

For the next couple of days you drift in and out of consciousness, feverish and often delirious from the effects of the virus, or the side effects of the medicine. Those who bring you food or come to examine you are always dressed in protective gear. You wonder what's going on in the outer world, but you don't even feel good enough to talk.

Then, a couple of days later, you awake feeling noticeably better. And extremely hungry! Your fever has broken. Three doctors are standing around you, and for the first time they're not wearing protective suits.

Turn ot page 29.

You're determined to find your classmates. You may get caught, but right now anything seems better than just moldering here on the floor. Ignoring the pain you feel with each step, you make it past the the sleeping guard and enter a long hallway with offices on either side. Near the end of the hall is a sign that says Cafeteria. You hear a noise—it sounds like someone crying. Probably this is where your classmates are being held. You realize how much you want to see Ms. Sealy and your friends.

You continue down the hall. When you get to within about fifty feet of the cafeteria, you stop to peer down a side corridor. The sign on the nearest door says Containment Room—Authorized Personnel Only. There's a little desk outside, perhaps for a guard, but right now no one's around.

"Halt!" A sharp voice from back toward the lobby sends a shot of adrenaline through your body. Maybe it's the guard who was asleep.

Should you obey? Or duck down the side corridor and try to find a place to hide?

*If you obey the order,
turn to page 16.*

*If you run down the side corridor,
turn to page 51.*

Other soldiers pour onto the institute's grounds, weapons drawn, obviously concerned that there may be more terrorists inside.

Most of the kids aren't concerned, however. They are yelling and cheering, waving at the window so they'll be seen.

"Let's get out of here!" someone shouts.

Ms. Sealy looks up. "Quiet down!" she calls in a stern voice. "We'll wait for a military escort. There may still be terrorists in the building."

Another personnel carrier races up the drive. More men jump out, dressed in white jumpsuits with white hoods and protective masks. They

look like astronauts. Several of them start talking into handheld radios. Others enter the building. A minute later they stream into the cafeteria. A cheer goes up. One of them talks with Ms. Sealy while the others stand near the door. Ms. Sealy turns on you, her face suddenly red with anger.

"Hey, let's go!" someone cries. Everyone is crowding toward the door.

Go on to the next page.

Ms. Sealy holds up her hands. "Just a minute! Apparently the vial holding the EF1 virus was broken. That's why the terrorists surrendered— they were terrified of being infected if they stayed inside the building."

Turn to page 48.

"Come!" orders the guard, pointing to the institute building. You limp along. The dog falls in at your heels.

The guard marches you through the lobby and shoves you into a windowless office, slamming the door behind you.

You pull off your sneaker and sock. Your ankle is caked with blood, and fresh blood oozes out of the wound.

Another terrorist, a slim woman with a hard, expressionless face who wears the same style of battle fatigues as the men, comes in.

"I need a doctor," you say.

She utters a sound of disgust, as if somehow you're the one at fault.

"I need water, too," you add.

Ignoring you, she walks out of the room. Maybe she doesn't speak English. You're left there, blood still trickling down your ankle onto the rug.

Turn to page 73.

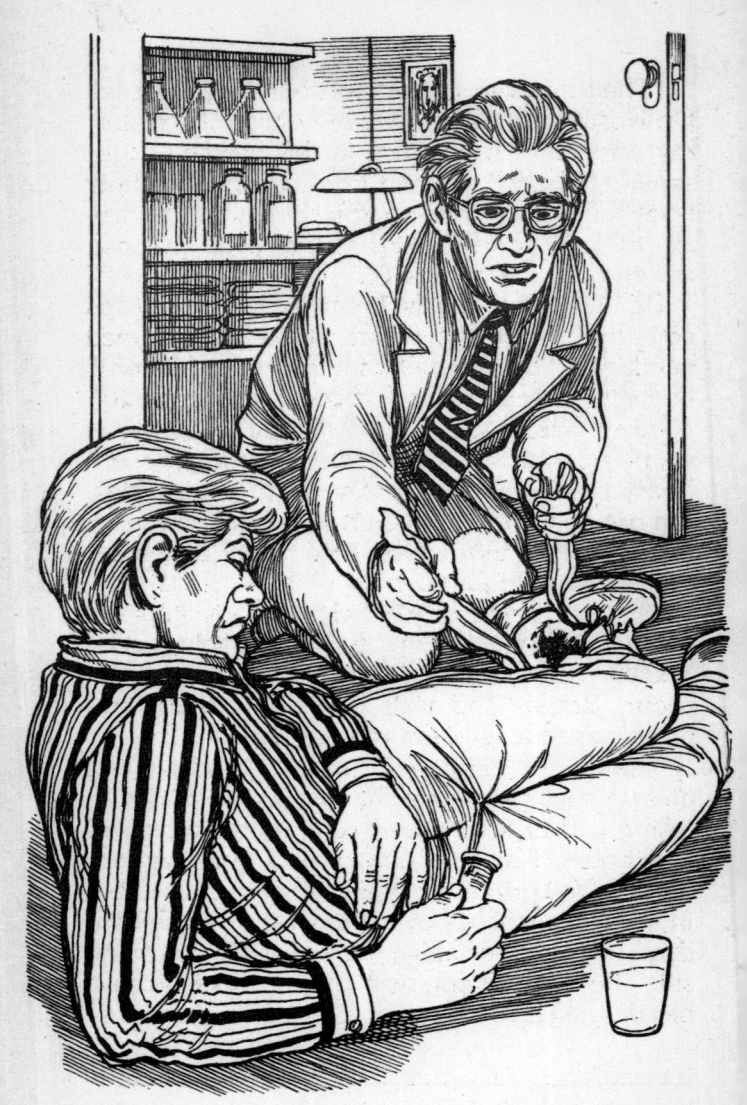

"They hijacked my school tour bus," you tell Dr. Kostrikis. "I think they're holding the rest of my classmates someplace in this building. I got separated because I tried to escape. That's how I got this." You point to your ankle. "I was trying to find the other kids, but a guard grabbed me and put me in here."

Dr. Kostrikis kneels beside you. He clasps your leg and gently unwraps the bloodstained bandage. "You're developing a nasty infection," he says. "Was it treated? It doesn't look like it."

You shake your head. "Well, you're lucky you stumbled into this office," the doctor goes on. "Bacterial infections are one of my specialties. I'm not equipped to stitch that wound, but I can treat you with antibiotics. And that's something we should do right now."

He goes back into his closet. This time he leaves the door open and turns on a light inside. You can see it's more than a closet—it's a storeroom. Bottles and vials line the shelves, and there's even a sink and refrigerator.

The doctor brings you a glass of water and gives you a shot. He hands you some pills, telling you to take one now and another every four hours. Then he goes to work cleaning your wound. You grimace in pain as he touches it, but in a few seconds it's over. He wraps a fresh bandage around your ankle. "It's best for you to lie still," he says. "If you walk around, it could start bleeding again."

Turn to page 11.

Soon afterward, two doctors garbed head to toe in protective clothing enter the room. They do what they can to save you, even injecting you with a newly developed medicine. Unfortunately, they're too late. The virus is too advanced in your body. You never leave the institute alive.

For that reason you never get to hear the good news. Every terrorist was killed or captured, and not a single other hostage was hurt. Perhaps most important, the killer virus was never released. You were the only person who became infected.

Later the president is criticized for ordering the special forces to attack, even though the operation was almost a complete success. Critics point out that the virus might have been released into the atmosphere, and millions of lives were at risk.

Turn to page 34.

"You're mighty lucky to be alive," one of them says. "You not only survived the killer virus, you also survived the drug we developed to combat it."

"I'm feeling much better," you say happily. You're excited just to be breathing, talking, and almost ready to sit up in bed.

"Some people think it was irresponsible of you to break that window and risk infecting others," the doctor adds. "But if it was, you've certainly suffered enough for it, serving as a medical guinea pig. Your job now is to get well enough to get out of here by a week from today. The president has invited you and all the kids who were held hostage for a tour of the White House. You'll even get to look in on the Oval Office."

"I've heard that before," you say.

"I know," the doctor replies. "Well, this time you can believe it."

The End

You race to the log and drag it toward the wall. It's heavier than you imagined, and it takes you precious seconds to get it there. When you lean the log up against the wall, it slides off. You try again, this time setting it more firmly on the ground. You think you've been quiet, but the dog must have heard you. It's racing toward you now, barking.

You scramble up the log, plant one foot on the top end, and swing your other leg and one arm over the wall. You're about to push off when you feel a stabbing pain—the dog sinking its teeth into your leg! Screaming, you try to pull your leg up, but the dog has a firm grip. It keeps yanking, trying to drag you down.

You are astride the top of the wall with an attack dog hanging on to your dangling leg. You strain to pull the dog up or shake it off. No way. Your arm is slipping. The pain in your leg saps your strength. You close your eyes and grit your teeth, hoping against hope the dog will let go to get a better grip.

It does! The weight is suddenly gone! You heave yourself over the wall. Your momentum carries you off balance, and you fall to the ground on the other side.

Turn to page 53.

"I'll stick with you," you tell Marcos. "I like the idea of getting rich."

"You will, Champ," he says. "And if you show you can keep your cool, I'll teach you this business from the ground up."

"Someday maybe I'll be like you—and run operations all over the world."

He smiles for a second, then extends a fat forefinger under your nose. "That's good, to be ambitious," he says. "But don't get too greedy. Or—" He makes the motion of a knife slitting your throat.

In the days ahead you ride with Marcos in trucks and jeeps through forests and jungles and up rivers on outboard motorboats. About twenty security men and engineers follow. You have no idea where you're going, and you're sure the CIA doesn't either. Too much of the travel has been under cover of the forest canopy, and there have been decoys: trucks and jeeps going off on other roads.

It's too late now to change your mind about staying with Marcos, but for the moment you feel safe. Somehow you've gained his confidence. In fact, he seems to have taken a liking to you. He makes everyone call you Champ. As if you've become the terrorists' mascot.

Turn to page 93.

"But he will do this much," Gruenwald continues into the tape recorder. "If the terrorists at the institute surrender, he will guarantee them safe passage to wherever in the world they wish to go. The alternative is that our special forces will destroy them. They will die for nothing."

"This is the only offer we will make," the president adds. "We will give them twenty-four hours to respond. And that time will not be extended. Twenty-four hours exactly from the time you deliver the message."

The next half hour is taken up with your repeating the message until you've memorized every word. The fateful moment arrives. Two aides deliver you by jeep to the institute gate. You walk across the strip between the army rangers and the terrorist guards, and once again you are at the mercy of some of the most ruthless criminals in the world.

Turn to page 7.

No one criticizes you, however. In fact, you'll be remembered as a national hero. The president awards you the Medal of Honor posthumously, presenting it to your parents in an impressive ceremony on the White House lawn. The sad thing is that you can't be there to receive it yourself.

The End

You say nothing. You don't want to cooperate in the slightest if you can help it. On the other hand, you're excited at the thought that you might actually be let go. This could be your big chance. You've got to be sure not to spoil it. Then you remind yourself that you've got to stop thinking only about how you can save your own skin. You could make a difference in the outcome of this disaster. Maybe you could ask questions, find out something about the terrorists. Things the president and the FBI would be interested in.

Turn to page 114.

You point to the storeroom. "They went through there!"

The guard wheels and rushes to the storeroom. He turns the knob and opens the door, stepping deftly to one side. With a sudden motion he points his weapon in and fires. The *rat-tat-tat* of gunfire is accompanied by the sound of breaking glass and splitting wood.

When he discovers no one is in there, he'll no doubt turn back and shoot you the same way. You don't want to be around when he does!

You make a break for it. A *click* behind you tells you the guard is reloading his weapon, but you're already through the door. Dr. Kostrikis is running down the hall with the vial in his hand. That's all you see. You feel a ferocious yank as the guard pulls you back into the room with such force that you fall to the floor.

He levels his gun at you.

"No!" you cry. But his finger is already squeezing the trigger.

The End

The afternoon wears on. You crawl from one end of the thicket to the other, trying to get some idea of what's going on. Then you see that everyone is out of the bus. Guards are herding your classmates up the slope toward the institute. You're glad you're not with them. On the other hand, you're not exactly safe where you are.

Returning to the opposite side of the thicket, you see there's now only one guard patrolling. You watch as he walks up the slope toward the institute and disappears behind a clump of cedar trees. It would take you only a few seconds to reach the wall, perhaps half a minute to drag the log over, set it up as a ramp, and escape. Maybe you should try it now. Or should you wait for darkness?

*If you try to scale the wall now,
turn to page 30.*

*If you decide to wait for darkness,
turn to page 14.*

You think about this a moment. Marcos must think he is making you a generous offer. Life with his band would certainly be exciting, but it would also be incredibly dangerous. And all the riches you'd make would be at the expense of innocent people. You could never agree to stay with this madman for your own benefit, but you have another motive. He still has the duplicate vial of the killer virus. If you agree to stay with him, you might get the chance to notify the American government about his whereabouts. Perhaps you might even steal the virus back from him. By sticking it out with him, you could be a mole, a spy for your country!

If you accept Marcos's offer to let you go home, turn to page 71.

If you decide to stay with him, turn to page 31.

"Give it to me," says the guard, holding out his hand. "Easy does it. Hand it over." They haven't noticed the vial on the desk. They obviously think you have the real one.

You hold the vial over the hard tile floor. "Come one step closer and I'll drop it," you say.

Half-smiling, the guard says, "No, you won't. You don't want to die." He steps closer, his hand extended a few feet from you.

He edges closer still.

By now you're desperate. "You want the vial?" you shout. "Well, here it is!" You hurl it to the floor. Glass splinters fly in all directions. A slightly purplish liquid begins spreading over the tiles. You want them to think you're crazy, so you burst into fiendish laughter. They run down the hall screaming, holding their noses, their only thought to avoid the deadly virus!

Your ruse worked. Now you've only got to hide the real vial—the one with the EF1 virus. It's still in plain view on the desk.

Maybe you should put it in the storeroom where Dr. Kostrikis was hiding—the guard has already shot it up, so they probably won't look there again. Or maybe you should keep the vial in your pocket and run to the cafeteria, where you're almost certain your classmates are being held.

If you put the vial in your pocket and run to the cafeteria, turn to page 82.

If you decide to put it in the storeroom, turn to page 89.

The woman grunts. She unrolls a bandage and binds the wound, tying a knot to hold the bandage together. She gives you a pat on your hip. "Toilet room," she says, and points to a door. She walks out without another word.

You look at the crudely wrapped bandage. *At least it will stop the bleeding,* you think. But you know it's not proper medical treatment.

Later someone brings you a couple of bagels and more water. The door is closed on you. You listen for the click of a lock but don't hear it. They probably think you're too disabled to wander off.

The evening wears on. You drift off to sleep. Later, when you get up to go to the bathroom, you find that it hurts to walk. You're glad to lie down again.

You lie there thinking of what must be going on—the threats, the anxious meetings at the White House. Most of all you think of your classmates and Ms. Sealy.

Go on to the next page.

You feel scared, you're in pain, but most of all you're lonely. You get up and walk to the door. As you suspected, it's not locked. You open it a crack and peer into the lobby. A guard is hunched over the reception desk, snoring loudly.

There's no way you can escape the compound—not with those dogs around. But you'd at least like to find your classmates. If you get caught in the meantime, they will probably just lock you in your room. You wouldn't be much worse off than you are now. On the other hand, walking is painful and probably bad for your ankle. Maybe you'd better just rest.

*If you decide to stay put,
turn to page 77.*

*If you try to find your classmates,
turn to page 21.*

Marcos taps his fingers on his desk. "Okay, Champ," he says. "You're going to see the president. You're going to tell him that he has until noon tomorrow to free those political prisoners and give all of them, and us, safe passage to where we want to go. And just to make sure he keeps his side of the bargain, we'll take the virus with us." With a little laugh, he adds, "Tell him that we can guard it better than he can. And tell him that if he doesn't like this plan, he's going to get a busload of kids back on his hands, all infected with the EF1 virus."

"If that's what you want to say, why don't you say it yourself?"

"Because you'll say it better," he snaps back. He lunges at you and before you can back away slaps your cheeks between his palms. He orders the guards, "Send the Champ to the White House."

Turn to page 64.

You hang on to the wheel, turning it to keep the boat in midstream as the river veers sharply to the right. In a moment you're around the bend and out of the line of fire. You pull up your shirt. The bullet grazed you, but nothing vital appears to have been injured.

You ease back the throttle, confident that none of Marcos's other boats can catch you. A glance at the fuel gauge tells you there's plenty in the tank. You'll probably be able to reach a village downstream.

Go on to the next page.

A few minutes later you hear a noise over-head. A helicopter zooms in on you—probably the terrorists coming to get you! You wrench the wheel over hard, hoping to get some protection from the overhanging branches along the shore. There's no chance you can escape into the dense jungle, and where would you go if you did?

The helicopter descends until it's hovering over the water just a few yards away.

You're a sitting duck. But no one's firing!
They're coming to get you, lowering a raft. In a
moment you learn who they are—CIA agents!
A minute later strong arms pull you aboard the
chopper. At last you're safe. And so is the vial
with the killer virus!

The End

48

A dozen kids start talking at once, but Ms. Sealy silences everyone with a single sharp clap of her hands. "The terrorists will all be quarantined," she says. "But so will we. Hopefully, we haven't caught the virus. But we may have, so the authorities have to protect against our spreading it to others." Then, turning to you and lowering her voice, she says, "They say you broke the vial. How could you have done such a thing?"

"But I didn't! And no one's infected," you protest. "The EF1 virus is still in its vial—here!"

You pull the vial out of your pocket. Everyone looks at you. A few of your classmates standing near you step back. One of the men in white jumpsuits takes the vial from your outstretched hand.

"What's this?" he says, cradling it with great care. "The terrorists told us you broke the EF1 vial."

"This is the real thing," you say. "I broke a fake vial to scare them away."

Ms. Sealy stares at you wide-eyed for a moment, then takes your arm. "If this is true, why then . . . you're a hero," she says.

You grin at her. "Then I guess I am."

Turn to page 112.

Call it bravery, call it foolishness, but you're determined to go back. "I'll do it, Mr. President," you say.

He leaps from his chair and shakes your hand. "You are a brave young man," he says. "I'm looking forward to presenting you with the Medal of Honor—" He almost adds "if," but cuts himself off. You know why: "If" may not happen. There is no assurance you will ever leave the institute alive.

The president nods at Gruenwald, the secretary of defense.

"All right," Gruenwald says, making sure he has your attention. "Here's what we want you to tell Marcos. Listen carefully. Ready?"

"Ready," you say.

He nods and starts a tape recorder on the table before him. Speaking slowly and carefully, he says, "We want you to tell Marcos that the president was very firm; that he said he can't release the forty-seven terrorist prisoners because he knows that if he did so, there would soon be forty-seven more terrorists in the world, masterminding forty-seven more schemes to bring misery and ruin on innocent people. And that they would think that, as long as they had a big enough weapon, they could get away with anything. So the president won't release the prisoners no matter what threats are made."

Turn to page 32.

50

Trying to sound sincere, you say, "I'm thinking about how amazing it is the way you guys have faked out so many governments—and now even the United States! You've got a lot of guts."

He looks at you awhile, as if trying to decide whether you're on the level. Finally he says, "So, you think we're pretty smart guys, eh?"

"Yeah, I do," you say.

He lets out something between a snicker and a laugh, then gets up, goes to the door, and opens it. For the next few minutes you can hear him and Arnoff talking, though you can't make out what they're saying. When he returns, he give you a hard look. "All right, Champ. Since you think so highly of us, you'll be interested in learning more about our methods. As a matter of fact, you can be a big help to us."

"How do you mean?"

"We can't be sure the virus in that vial is really the killer virus until we test it."

"How will you do that?"

"It's easy," he says in a friendly tone. "You will be our test."

"What do you mean by that?"

He doesn't answer. The guards he buzzed for have arrived, two rough-looking men and a woman, all in combat gear. Marcos gestures at them. "They'll show you."

Turn to page 109.

You run down the side corridor.

"Halt!" the terrorist yells, but you dart around another corner. The corridor ahead comes to a dead end. You duck into an office. A second later you hear the steps of the guard running by. He'll figure out where you went soon enough. You've got to get out fast!

You smash the window with a chair and jump through, landing in a large bush nestled against the building. Branches and twigs break your fall, and you land without breaking any bones. But the impact leaves you scratched and bruised and opens up your wound, bringing on fresh waves of pain in your ankle. You scramble into a thicket. A second later you hear bullets splitting branches in the bushes around you.

You hunker down for a second or two and then start crawling through the shrubbery planted along the foundation. You stop for a moment to look up at the window. There's no sign of the guard who was firing at you. That's a relief. Except maybe he's coming down to look for you.

You can't move much from where you are. But just ahead is a wooden shed attached to the institute. Maybe you can hide there.

Turn to page 12.

Now not just your ankle but your whole body hurts! But strong arms are lifting you—the arms of army rangers. They load you onto a stretcher. Less than a minute later you're in an ambulance on your way to the hospital. Even in your pain, you're happy. You did it! You escaped!

Now you have to start worrying about your friends, and maybe a lot more people besides.

The End

"I'm not so sure he will," Marcos says with a sly smile. "Because I will be keeping the vial with the killer virus to make sure there's no treachery. You see, Champ, I don't trust your president any more than he trusts me."

You're crestfallen when you hear this. There is no way the president will let Marcos take that virus. You try to protest, but at a snap of Marcos's fingers, the guards seize you.

Once again you are returned to your room. There you sit, like all hostages: helpless, waiting. If only you could do something!

You look around the room. There's a ventilation duct in one corner of the ceiling. You hear a faint sound coming through it. There are two little steel chairs in the room, and you push one under the duct and stand on it. Then, to get even higher, you plant your feet on the arms of the chair, balancing carefully to keep from falling off. You hold your ear close to the duct and hear a voice. It's Marcos, speaking excitedly. Then you hear another voice you don't recognize.

Go on to the next page.

"So you see, Marcos, in the space of a few minutes we have done what you were afraid we couldn't do—we have successfully separated the EF1 virus. We now have two vials, each with the same deadly contents!"

"You're sure nothing escaped?" Marcos asks nervously.

"Absolutely sure."

"Ha! Well done, Arnoff. Well done! This means we can return the virus and keep it as well!"

"Exactly."

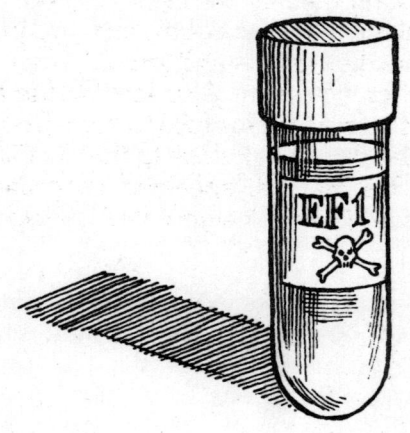

Turn to page 79.

"The terrorists are all in custody," one of the men answers. "When you broke that window, army rangers were planning how to mount an assault. The terrorists saved them the trouble—they panicked at your little stunt and ran right into the arms of our waiting troops. No one was hurt, and we recovered the killer virus still sealed in its vial. We have it under tight security."

"That's great," you say.

"Maybe." His face is stone cold. "Breaking that window helped us overtake the terrorists, but it also broke the quarantine of this room. You may be infected. The guard nearest the window may have become infected. He may infect others. This killer virus could get completely out of hand. It will be a couple of days before we know."

He turns abruptly. "The doctor will be with you soon."

The two men leave. You hear them lock the door behind them. It's a horrible sound—you've been rescued, but you're just as much a prisoner as you were when you were being held by the terrorists!

The doctor arrives a few minutes later, accompanied by one of the institute scientists. They are both wearing masks and protective suits. It's pretty obvious they think you're dangerous. The doctor examines you briefly and then gives you a shot.

Turn to page 20.

You writhe and cry out as if you're out of your mind, hoping the guard won't realize you're trying to distract him.

He comes over and stares at you, obviously confused. "Shut up!" he yells, and to emphasize the point, he gives you a kick in the side. Now your writhing is real, but you hold back the scream building inside you. You don't want another kick like that!

Go on to the next page.

You watch him out of the corner of your eye, wondering whether Dr. Kostrikis has been able to get the vial. As if reading your thoughts, the guard suddenly turns and runs out the door. A moment later you hear him yelling.

"Halt! Freeze!" He must have spotted Dr. Kostrikis! You struggle to your feet and follow until you can see around the corner. Your heart sinks. The guard has his gun trained on Dr. Kostrikis, who is cringing against the wall, holding the vial in his hand. Bad luck. If only he'd had a second or two more, he could have ducked down a side corridor!

The guard moves toward him. "Put vial very gently on floor!" he commands.

Dr. Kostrikis nods, but instead of doing as the guard orders, he slides the vial along the floor toward him. It careens along, angling toward the wall. With a gasp, the guard rushes toward it and stops it with his outstretched palms. In that instant, Dr. Kostrikis vanishes around the corner.

Turn to page 10.

You decide to stay on the bus. Ann Stoddart is still listening to her radio. You lean over toward her, and she holds it so you can hear, too. Ms. Sealy is coming up the aisle, trying to get kids to keep calm. She stops and listens. Others crowd around. You strain to hear every word:

For those who just tuned in, we'll bring you up to date. A band of about twenty terrorist paramilitaries directed by the Alarin crime cartel has seized the Biological Research Institute in Washington, D.C. At this moment army, police, and FBI units surround the five-acre institute compound. Orders have not been given for them to move in because the terrorists have hijacked a tour bus with thirty-two students on it and driven it onto the grounds. They have threatened to kill the students if any move is made against them.

This would be bad enough as it is, but by seizing the institute the terrorists, in a sense, hold the entire country hostage! The deadly EF1 virus, which scientists have been using for research, lies in a vault inside the institute.

Go on to the next page.

The terrorists have demanded that forty-seven of the most notorious international criminals be released from jail. Two of these are nerve gas scientists who have worked in the past for terrorists; one is a leading expert on plastic explosives; another is a powerful guerrilla leader. The terrorists say that unless these walking threats to world peace and stability are released within seventy-two hours, they will let the virus loose.

The consequences of such an event would be ghastly. The EF1 kills within hours and is more contagious than the virus for the common cold. The plague could spread across the country, and then perhaps the world. Millions could die. Further events in this grave crisis will be reported as soon as we learn of them.

"Why aren't you in your seats?" a voice cries in a foreign accent. The terrorist has returned, brandishing his weapon. You all scramble to your seats. There's a burst of gunfire so close it hurts your ears. You look up and see shafts of sunlight streaming through bullet holes in the roof. The terrorist grabs Ann's radio and smashes it to the floor.

Turn to page 107.

Ann looks at you blankly for a moment, then says, "Yes. There's a killer virus kept in that building. They've been using it for research, but it's extremely contagious, and the terrorists are threatening to let it out!"

So that's what's going on, you think. *All the more reason to get out of here!*

There's a concrete wall about six feet high that appears to surround the property of the institute. If you could get to it, you could probably find a way to boost yourself up and over. You should have no problem getting out of the bus. Ms. Sealy has moved to the back, where she's trying to get some kid to stop crying.

At that moment Liam Neilson taps your shoulder. He whispers, "If it weren't for that guard, we could escape over the wall."

"I was thinking the same thing," you whisper back.

Turn to page 67.

Several hours pass. It will soon be dark. Nothing much happens except that a new female terrorist boards the bus with two jugs of water and a couple of bags of bagels. She gives them to Ms. Sealy and the driver to distribute.

Bagels and water. It looks like this will be your diet for a while.

You see two more terrorists running down the drive. They speak to the man guarding you in their own language. He comes up to you.

"Okay, Champ," he says. "Tell the students they are being taken up to the building. They will be kept in the cafeteria."

You do as he says, feeling very uncomfortable. Why aren't they giving the orders themselves, instead of telling you to? It's as if they enjoy making you work for them. *Well,* you think, *there are worse things they could do.*

You are instructed to order everyone on the bus to walk to the building. As you are about to join the others being marched off like prisoners of war, the guard blocks your way.

"You're coming with me," he says. Grasping your elbow, he propels you into a side entrance, then up a flight of stairs to the second floor.

You've been scared all along, but at least you were with your friends. Now you can feel yourself sweating, your pulse racing. Why have you been singled out like this? Maybe to be shot or tortured as an example?

Turn to page 85.

The terrorists take you in a jeep to the front gate, then let you out and tell you to run across the road. You're only too eager to obey. In a few moments you're in the midst of army rangers. You tell them all that's gone on and all that you've learned. An armed escort rushes you to the White House; then aides escort you to the Situation Room, several floors below ground. A seat is provided for you at a large, oblong table. In attendance are some of the president's top advisers.

This has all happened so fast, it's hard to take in. One minute you were a terrorist prisoner,

and the next you are about to meet the president of the United States! And suddenly here he is, walking into the room, looking drawn and tired. You've never seen him except on television, when he's made up like an actor going onstage.

He immediately comes up to you and shakes your hand. "How are you feeling?"

Go on to the next page.

"A lot better than I was," you answer.

"Good. I want to get you back with your family as soon as possible, but first I need to ask for your help." He gives you a quick smile. "All right?"

"Sure," you say.

"Good. First, tell us everything you observed."

Turn to page 110.

A minute later a military helicopter roars overhead. Thousands of little pieces of paper fill the air in its wake. You guess they are leaflets, urging the terrorists to surrender. The man guarding the bus gets to his feet and watches the papers fluttering down. He starts after one. This could be your chance. In the time it takes him to catch and read the leaflet, you could race to a nearby clump of bushes and hide. Then, when the coast is clear, you could escape over the wall!

The guard is running now, his hand outstretched as the piece of paper above him blows in the wind.

If you make a break for the clump of bushes, turn to page 101.

If you stay on the bus, turn to page 60.

A couple of pickup trucks are parked by the shack that serves for a terminal building, along with a number of jeeps and other vehicles in a dirt lot beyond. Marcos is standing nearby, talking to some men in camouflage gear.

A Land Rover pulls up alongside the plane. A man wearing blue jeans and a T-shirt gets out and gives Marcos a military-style salute, which he returns with a little wave of his hand.

Marcos comes over to you, a smug expression on his face. "I insisted that the president let me take you this far so I could be sure I wouldn't be shot down on the way. There's no way they'll know where I'm going next. There are many roads leading from this strip. They run through the rain forest and are not visible from the air. Tomorrow at this time I'll be hundreds of miles away in whatever direction I choose."

"So you'll let me go?"

"Why not?" he answers. "You're of no further use to me. You were just my final bit of insurance, to make sure I got this far without being harmed. So, if you want to go back, you're free to do so. But if you'll think about it, maybe you won't want to go. I'm impressed with you, kid. You're brave and you're smart. You could have a great future in our organization. Your life could be far more interesting. You could be rich beyond your dreams. So, if you are as smart as I think you are, you may join us. The choice is yours."

Turn to page 39.

The door is made of heavy steel. There's no chance of breaking out, but you could move your bed under the window facing the hallway, then climb up and break the window with the chair. That might send the terrorists into panic, and maybe you could find a way to escape.

Then again, if you *are* contagious, breaking the window might mean letting the virus loose throughout the whole building, maybe even throughout the whole population of Washington!

If you decide to break the window, turn to page 104.

If you decide it's too risky, turn to page 17.

"I want to go home," you say.

"Suit yourself," he says with a shrug. He starts to go.

"How do I get out of here?" you ask.

"Just hang around. A CIA plane will land soon. They know you're here. They will pick you up. They'll sniff around here like hound dogs for a few hours, but it won't do them any good. You'll be on your way home pretty quick."

At that moment a truck pulls up, and Marcos climbs aboard without another word. The truck accelerates, spewing diesel fumes, and disappears into the jungle, followed by the other vehicles that were parked at the airstrip. Almost immediately afterward, the plane that brought you takes off, leaving you completely alone.

You spend an anxious hour waiting before the CIA plane lands. Several agents climb out, and after checking to see that you're all right, they comb the airstrip and the building, just as Marcos predicted, before taking off with you aboard.

Turn to page 74.

You and the terrorist whirl around. A line of assault rifles is leveled on him. The army rangers have arrived!

One of them motions for you to get away from the terrorist. You quickly step aside. With the lightning moves of a martial arts master, the ranger collars the terrorist, disarms him, swings him around, and has him in handcuffs almost faster than the eye can see.

You grip the vial carefully with both hands. Gradually it dawns on you that the ordeal is over. The killer virus didn't get loose. The terrorists have been foiled. And you're not a hostage anymore!

The End

You wiggle along the floor until you can raise your leg and rest it on a chair. That should slow the bleeding. It's not so bad that you need a tourniquet—you're not going to bleed to death. You lie back and close your eyes, wondering where your classmates are, wondering if you'll ever get out of this alive.

Another woman comes in. This one is short, dark complexioned, and has a nice face despite a crescent-shaped scar that runs across her cheek. She hands you a glass of water and walks out. A few minutes later she comes back, carrying a first aid kit.

"No speak English," she says, and bends over your ankle, inspecting your wound.

Turn to page 42.

On the way back to the States, you tell the CIA agents what you know, including the fact that Marcos's chief scientist succeeded in making a duplicate of the virus. Then they give you some astonishing news. Marcos never had the real virus! A scientist at the institute was able to substitute a fake one before the terrorists got to it. Marcos doesn't know it, but if he and his friends decide to let loose the virus they have in their possession, the most they'll be able to do is give a few people the flu.

"This is great news," you say.

"Yes, it is," one of the agents replies. "But we can't exactly throw a party to celebrate. The Alarin cartel is still intact. And some of the most daring and brilliant terrorists in the world are still on the loose."

The End

Your schoolmates are all there, with a terrorist guard standing over them. Some are sitting at cafeteria tables, some are lying down. Some kids wave when they see you. Others just stare at you blankly as if they've lost hope. Everyone looks exhausted. You can see fear in their eyes.

Turn to page 99.

You decide to stay put. It would be nice to have company, but trying to move around could open up your wound. Besides, you probably wouldn't get very far before you got caught. You lie there, wishing you were home or in a hospital, or anywhere else but here. Tired as you are, it's hard to go to sleep. Your ankle feels worse. You're sure it's infected. You just hope you'll be rescued soon.

You spend a restless night, drifting in and out of consciousness. The following morning you wake up feeling worse than ever. Your ankle is throbbing. You can tell it's infected. You feel hot and dry, as if you're burning up. You open your eyes and then close them against the glare of light. Your head aches. You try to move, but you feel terribly weak.

In the hours that follow, the terrorists look in on you from time to time. They bring you water and stale bagels but show no interest in treating your infection, which is getting steadily worse.

The day wears on. You didn't bring a watch, and you've lost track of time. You're dozing when you're jolted by the sound of an explosion, then the *rat-tat-tat-tat-tat-tat* of gunfire. You smell smoke. Men are yelling. There is another explosion. More shouts. You lean on one elbow, trying to raise yourself, wondering what's going on. But as if that little effort was more than you could take, you slump back on the floor. A moment later you pass out.

Turn to page 19.

He returns a few moments later. "Bad news. The guard has returned." He looks at you with a sly smile. "But I think we can overcome that problem."

"But there's no way you can get past him," you say.

"Not if he's there. But maybe he won't be there," Dr. Kostrikis says with a wink.

"Why not?"

"Because you will have distracted him—and you don't even need to move. After I leave, count ten seconds. On the count of ten, let out a scream and yell, 'Don't shoot! Don't shoot!' The guard will come running. Just keep him busy for half a minute—that's all I'll need."

"Okay, but—"

"You don't have to do it if you don't want to," Dr. Kostrikis says.

"But what will you do with the vial?"

"Hide it where they can't find it."

"Where?"

"I don't know, but I'll think of a place. I know this building inside out."

You have your doubts about whether Dr. Kostrikis's plan will work, but you agree to go along with it.

He gives you a reassuring pat on the shoulder. "Thanks," he says. "Start counting when I walk through the door."

Turn to page 92.

You hop down and return the chair to its place. There's too much risk of you being caught if you stay up there; but you've already heard enough. You consider what it means. There is no way the president will let Marcos take the killer virus. But now he'll think that Marcos has surrendered the virus, not knowing he has another sample. Marcos may get away with the killer virus after all and hold the world hostage another day!

The hours ahead are filled with confusion. Guards blindfold you; then you have the sense of being led someplace, then riding in some kind of vehicle. After that, you're led on foot some distance and put on an airplane. You hear the sound of the plane's engines, then feel the acceleration as it takes off.

Your questions to the men guarding you go unanswered. You can guess what's happening, however. Marcos has accepted the president's offer, fooling him just as you feared. And although your classmates have probably been let go as part of the deal, Marcos has somehow been able to keep you as hostage.

Hours pass. When the plane finally lands and the door is opened, warm, sultry air drifts in. Someone leads you out of the plane and onto a tarmac. Only then is your blindfold removed, and you can see where you are: on a tiny airstrip carved out of the jungle. Judging by how long the flight lasted, you're probably somewhere in South America.

Turn to page 69.

You're lying in a hospital bed, recovering from an infection caused by the dog bite, when you look up and are startled to see the president of the United States!

"Gosh, sir," you say. "I never thought you'd have time to visit *me.*"

"It's true that I'm busier than usual these days," he says. "But I wanted to stop by and pay my respects. You played an important part in thwarting the terrorists."

"I thought all I did was escape."

"That was quite a feat in itself," the president says. "And when you came barreling down the grounds of the institute in that tractor, you took the terrorists by surprise. Maybe they thought you were getting away with the EF1 virus. Some of them chased you, and those who didn't watched through the windows. That distraction was all our rangers needed. They landed our helicopters on the roof, blew open a hole, dropped down, secured the building, and rescued all the hostages in about thirty-five seconds. We had every one of the terrorists in custody a few minutes later!"

"That's terrific," you say.

He gives you a broad grin. "I can't stay any longer," he says. "But I'll see you next week when you come to the White House."

"I'm coming to the White House?"

"You bet. So I can present you with the Medal of Honor."

The End

You carefully place the vial in a front pocket of your jeans and start running toward the cafeteria. In your excitement you forget your bad ankle. With the first running step, your wound opens, jolting you with pain so bad you have to keep yourself from crying out.

A terrorist guard runs out of the cafeteria, leaving the door ajar. You're afraid he'll shoot you, but he runs past, looking just as frightened as you are. You stagger inside the cafeteria. Your classmates are all there. You hardly recognize some of them. They look strained and tired, as if they've been held prisoner for weeks!

Ms. Sealy and the bus driver turn around, startled to see you. Ms. Sealy hurries toward you.

"Hey, look!" a kid peering out the window yells.

Everyone runs over to see. You limp along with them. Out in the yard, eight men and three women—the terrorists—are walking toward the front gate, their hands in the air. Army personnel carriers and tanks are pouring over the grounds. Soldiers in camouflage gear jump out and train their rifles on the terrorists. You watch with amazement and joy as they are herded onto a bus.

Turn to page 22.

You open the box, take the vial, stuff it into the front pocket of your jeans, and close the box again. You back out into the hallway and look around. No one has seen you. You walk down the hall, up the steps, and into the office area. The women working their computers hardly glance at you, but there's a guard standing at the entrance. Through the opening you see that a motorboat has pulled up to the dock. Men are unloading supplies, including a heavy steel box that looks very much like the safe Marcos is waiting for. The boat has larger outboard engines than the one you arrived in—it's almost certainly the fastest one at the dock.

"Where do you think you're going?" the guard says as you approach the entrance.

"Marcos wanted me to give a message to the boatman."

"What message?" He tenses, his hand touching his holster.

"He wants to talk to him before he goes back," you say, thinking fast.

The guard relaxes. "You don't need to. We already told him."

"I think he *wants* to tell him twice," you say. "Understand?"

You're afraid that what you're saying sounds phony. But the guard evidently isn't very bright. He gives you a wink and motions you to pass.

Turn to page 88.

You pass a window at the landing—you long to jump through it, you'd do anything to escape, but there's no way.

The guard takes you up to the door of an office. A plaque on it reads CONFERENCE ROOM. He opens the door.

"In there, Champ," he says, giving you a shove. It's semidark inside. There's a long wooden table with ten or twelve chairs around it. A middle-aged, heavyset man dressed in camouflage gear and wearing an olive drab cap sits at one end of the table, talking on a cellular phone. His pale face is pitted with scars.

"Sit down." He gestures and resumes talking into the phone, so softly you can't make out what he's saying. He hangs up and talks with your guard in a foreign language, then looks back at you.

"I am Marcos. And you are *Champ,* right?"

"That's what he calls me," you say, indicating the guard.

"So, Champ you will be," Marcos says. "You've done your first job okay. We have another one for you."

You stand silently—with no idea what to say.

"First I want you to come look at your friends." He motions to the guard, who wheels you around and then leads you down the hall into the cafeteria.

Turn to page 76.

"Oh, no. The terrorists never got their hands on it," the doctor says warmly. "We'll bring you the morning newspaper—you can read all about it."

"Great—but what about my classmates?" you ask anxiously. "Is everyone okay?"

"Not a single hostage was killed or seriously injured," he answers. "Some of your friends are a little worse for wear, but they'll all be okay. The virus is safely locked up. And so are the terrorists!"

The End

The president leans toward you. "I would never suggest it if this weren't an extremely grave crisis, with possibly millions of lives at stake if that virus gets out. Even so, I am not ordering you to go back. I don't even want to *ask* you. You're certainly not old enough to be drafted. Just say the word and you'll be on your way home. It's your decision. We'll have a special escort take you home if you want, but . . ." His voice trails off.

"But?" you ask.

"But the fact is, we think Marcos will be more likely to let down his guard if we have you as a go-between rather than an adult he doesn't know. That's why we're willing to ask you."

Your mind is spinning. You're unable to answer.

"Take a few minutes to decide," the president says.

You wish that you had more than a few minutes. You want to do whatever you can. You'd like to be a hero. On the other hand, you don't want to be a dead hero!

If you volunteer to go back to the institute, turn to page 49.

If you decide not to go, turn to page 15.

The boatman has unloaded all his supplies. A woman is signing a paper to show that the goods were delivered. You stand nearby, waiting for a chance to talk to him. He takes the clipboard and looks at you.

"Excuse me," you say. "Marcos sent me to tell you he wants to see you."

"Sure, sure, I know," he says impatiently. Holding the clipboard with the signed receipts, he follows the woman toward the office.

You're left alone. The guard at the entrance follows them inside. The boat is tied to the dock, its lines looped around a couple of cleats. Your eyes fall on the control panel. The key is in the ignition. You'll never have a chance like this again!

You unwrap the lines and leap into the boat, turn the switch, and give it some throttle. The engine roars to life. You slip it in gear and are thrown off your feet as the boat accelerates with astonishing speed. You hear yelling onshore. Bullets fly past you, leaving a line of holes in the hull. You recover the wheel barely in time to avoid slamming into the riverbank. Muddy brown waves from your wake slap against the gnarled mangrove roots along the shore.

Once on course, you give the boat full throttle, heading downstream. You weave wildly, almost losing control. Bullets whip past you. One glances off the compass bracket and sends shards of metal flying through the air. You're jolted aside by a stinging pain in your side.

Turn to page 45.

You head for the office where you met Dr. Kostrikis, intending to put the vial in the store-room. Before you get there, you come face-to-face with a terrorist—one of the guards who was there when you smashed the vial. Your heart sinks. You were hoping they all ran out of the building when you smashed the fake vial.

He gives you the most furious look you've ever seen in your life.

"Get away or you'll catch the virus!" you yell.

His voice is trembling. "I already caught it. I breathed that vapor. Maybe the virus will kill you, too. But I'm not going to take any chances." He trains his gun on you. Then his eyes widen as he notices the vial you're holding. "What's that? That couldn't be it, could it?" His mouth hangs open. You can practically hear the wheels turning in his head.

"Don't touch it—it's leaking!" you scream.

He stares anxiously.

"It's got on my hands," you say. "Get out while you still can!"

"Freeze!"

Turn to page 72.

Marcos inspects the box.

"The safe hasn't arrived," one of the guards says. "It should have come on the downstream boat that was due at noon. Where do you want to keep this in the meantime?"

Marcos mutters something under his breath. "I'll keep it here in my office. When that boat gets here, find out why it was late!"

"Yes, Marcos," the guards answer together. They turn to leave.

"And let me know when it arrives," Marcos yells after them. He wheels the cart into his office, which is right next to your room. A moment later he strides away, apparently not even caring that he's left the vial in an unlocked room.

Why would he be so careless? you wonder. It must be because no one would dare cross him. Except you! This could be your chance to escape with the vial!

Not much of a chance, you realize. The odds against getting the vial out of this place are slim. And the odds against getting it out of this jungle are probably even slimmer. On the other hand, what future is there for you here?

*If you try to get away with the vial,
turn to page 83.*

*If not,
turn to page 116.*

You watch as he opens the door a crack, then slips through.

You count silently. At ten, you start yelling. Seconds later the guard who shoved you into the room rushes in, waving his weapon, his eyes darting about. He fixes on you, shouting angrily in the same language you heard before, then in English, *"What you do?"* You cringe as he thrusts the cold steel muzzle of his gun against your neck. You see his finger tensing on the trigger. You're afraid that if you don't do something to distract him, he'll kill you!

If you point toward the storeroom door and say, "They went through there," turn to page 36.

If you writhe and cry out as if you're out of your mind, turn to page 57.

On the fourth day after you landed on the airstrip, you travel up a narrowing muddy river crowded by the jungle on both sides. About noon, the boat pulls up to a makeshift dock at the edge of an Indian village. Marcos's aide leads you into what looks like a thatched hut, but inside, instead of a dirt floor and mats to sit on, is a modern office with molded fiberglass desks and chairs, overhead lighting, computers, and other equipment. Several women wearing T-shirts and khaki shorts are sitting at computers. Marcos leads you past them, then down a flight of stairs to a level below ground. Ahead of you is a long hallway flanked by doors on either side.

Marcos opens one of them. Inside is a bunk, a chair, some open shelves, and not much else. "You'll sleep here, next to my office," he says. "I have some business to do. There's a pool table and some arcade games at the end of the hall if you want something to do."

A couple of guards come along, wheeling a cart. In the cart is a box cushioned with triple layers of bubble wrap. You're sure it contains the vial with the EF1 virus!

Turn to page 90.

You head for the gate anyway, at full throttle.
One of the guards aims at you. You duck. Bullets ping off your fender. You turn the tractor
sharply to try to dodge the next volley. Suddenly
there's a small explosion and you're enveloped
in a cloud of smoke. You can't see a thing. You
don't know where you're heading. You just try
to keep driving, coughing and gasping for air.
Then, through the thinning smoke, you see the
wall ahead. You swerve right. The smoke is
clearing. You see the gate! You're almost to it.
The grilled iron doors are chained shut, but you
put your head down, keep the throttle on full,
and drive straight into them! Steel meets iron.
The chain gives way. The doors fly open, and
suddenly you're out in the street!

You take your foot off the gas. The tractor
chugs to a stop a few feet from an army tank.
You try to get out, but you're too weak and
shaky to move.

A second later army rangers are pulling you
out. They lay you on a stretcher and start running for a military ambulance parked a few yards
down the street. The tank's forty-millimeter cannon swings around, aiming at the terrorist
guards who are standing by the gate. The message is clear. Virus or no virus, fire your
weapons and you'll be blown out of existence!

Turn to page 80.

You decide to play it straight and not come on with a phony line about admiring Marcos. You're pretty sure he would see right through you. Instead, you decide to simply say what's on your mind.

"I'm wondering why you're doing this," you say. "And why you don't care about the suffering you're causing, keeping all these innocent people hostage, and threatening to kill millions! Don't you have any feeling for other people?"

You're afraid Marcos will lash out at you. But he half-smiles and wryly shakes his head. "You're quite the philosopher, aren't you?" He leans toward you, making a fist and laying it up under your nose. "Understand this: My philosophy is to live well and to get what I want. That's all there is to it!"

You had thought that Marcos would try to justify his actions, claiming that there was some greater good to be achieved. But here he is admitting that cruelty and greed are just fine! This man and all his buddies need to be locked up for a long time. But you know that's not going to happen soon. Right now, Marcos is holding all the cards.

You are trying to think of some other tack you could take when several other terrorists enter the room and start talking with Marcos in their own language. You can't tell what they're saying, but you notice that everyone is nodding—they seem to be in agreement.

Turn to page 44.

In about a minute you reach the wall. You tilt the log up at a forty-five-degree angle, then try to jam the bottom end into the dirt so it won't topple over when you climb onto it. You scramble up the log, grab the top of the wall, and start to swing your leg over.

There's no barking, no growling, just the sudden terrible shock and searing pain of jaws locked on your left ankle. They pull you off balance, bringing you crashing to the ground, almost on top of the guard dog attacking you! The dog rolls on its side to keep clear, still gripping your ankle in its powerful jaws.

Someone runs toward you. You hear a command shouted in a foreign language. The dog releases your ankle but stands menacingly over you, a low, throaty growl warning you not to get up.

A terrorist guard runs up. He calls something to another man, then stands over you, clicking his fingers at the dog, which sits obediently.

"Stand up!" the guard commands. He's a square-shouldered, muscular man. You struggle to your feet, your ankle throbbing, your sock wet with blood.

Turn to page 25.

"Do you think the terrorists have the combination to the vault?"

"Probably not, but this isn't like some big bank vault. They could take the door off its hinges with an acetylene torch in about half a minute. Wouldn't do any damage to the vial. You can be sure they are very sophisticated about that sort of thing. Did you notice whether there was a guard at the desk outside the Containment Room?"

"There wasn't," you say.

"Ah. That's interesting. There was one before. I'm going to look around. I'll be right back."

You watch as Dr. Kostrikis opens the door a crack and peers out. The coast must be clear, because he slips out, quietly closing the door behind him.

Turn to page 78.

One boy is sobbing. Three younger kids are lying in a corner. Two of them look very pale—either they've been beaten or fallen ill. A guard is keeping anyone from helping them. An older girl is shivering. She lets out a cry that turns into a long, plaintive wail.

You start to go over to talk to Ms. Sealy, but the guard abruptly whips you away and marches you back toward the conference room. Marcos is waiting for you.

"You have seen your friends," he says. "They don't look too good, do they? They are going to look much worse. They are not going to get any more food or water. The president should know this. He should know that all those kids are going to die a horrible death unless he's willing to meet our demands."

"Why are you telling me this?" you ask.

"Because," he says with a smile, "you are going to take this message to the president. You will tell him you have seen how much your friends are suffering. This will help him understand."

Turn to page 35.

You lean back and whisper to Liam, "I'm making a break for it. If you want to come, let's go!"

You get to your feet. In a flash you're through the door and running, hoping to make the clump of bushes before you're seen.

Liam isn't with you. You glance back and see that the driver has collared him just as he was leaving the bus. You keep on running. A second later you dive into a thicket of leafy bushes. You're a little scratched, but you don't think the guard saw you. You crouch there, catching your breath, then crawl along until you reach the far edge of the thicket's protective cover. There's an open stretch of about fifty feet between the thicket and the wall, with a fallen log lying about halfway in between. You're pretty sure you could lean it up against the wall and use it as a ramp. But two terrorist guards are patrolling along the wall, each with a handheld radio and a guard dog on a leash. If you're going to get over the wall you'll have to do it fast, and probably at night.

You wait patiently, watching the guards walk back and forth. An occasional helicopter flies overhead. You'd think that by now the FBI or the army could have moved in and recaptured the institute, but it's obvious that no orders have been given to launch an assault.

Turn to page 38.

102

"Is there anything we can do?" you ask anxiously.

Dr. Kostrikis shakes his head. "No. Except . . ." He glances at the door. "It's a long shot, but . . ." He squats down and in a low voice goes on, "The EF1 is in a vial about fifty feet down the hall. It's in a steel vault inside what's called the Containment Room. I'm one of the few people who know the combination to the lock on the vault. I doubt if they've removed the vial. They wouldn't want to risk having the virus get out any more than anyone else. They'd be the first ones to die!"

"They want to keep it as a threat, like a nuclear bomb," you say.

Dr. Kostrikis nods. "Exactly."

Turn to page 98.

You understand only too well. There is nothing you can say. A few moments later they leave. You hear them lock the door. You stand helplessly in the middle of the room. It's going to be a long night. And by this time tomorrow you may be dead.

The evening wears on. You still feel pretty well. Maybe you're not infected after all. But if you are, by now you must be highly contagious. You look longingly at the door, wishing you could break it down. The terrorists would all run. They'd be afraid of catching the virus themselves.

Turn to page 70.

You stand on the bed and smash the window with the back of the steel chair. The guard outside yells. You're not quite tall enough to see through the broken pane, but you hear shouts and cries of *"Get out! Get out! The quarantine's broken!"*

Running footsteps. More shouts, farther away. Then silence. Your plan may have worked! But the window is too small for you to fit through and the door is still locked.

Twenty minutes pass before you hear anything else, but then loud noises erupt in the hall. You hear heavy footsteps and someone shouting. Suddenly the door opens. Two men come in, wearing protective white suits and masks. With them comes the smell of strong disinfectants.

One of them approaches you. "Do you feel all right?"

"I don't know," you say. "I may have the killer virus. They injected me."

"Let's hope not," he says. "Meanwhile, we'll have to keep you here under quarantine. We'll have that window sealed up in a couple of minutes. Don't try to break it again. We're going to leave you now, but a doctor will be here to look at you soon." They turn to leave.

"Have they captured the terrorists?" you ask. "Are the other kids okay?"

Turn to page 56.

Hours go by. It must be well after midnight. You're already drained by fatigue and anxiety, thinking you must be a fool to have come back. At last a guard looks in on you.

"Has Marcos decided what to do yet?"

He gives you a contemptuous look. "You'll know when he decides. But I'll tell you right now that the answer will not be 'yes.' It will either be 'no' or 'maybe.' If it's 'no,' he won't have you bring it to the president. He'll just send your body."

You squirm, hearing these brutal words. The guard smiles, as if your suffering is just what he wanted to see, then walks out, leaving you alone with your thoughts. He returns a few minutes later and beckons you to come with him, giving you no hint of what Marcos's decision will be.

Turn to page 115.

"This time bullets through the roof, next time through one of you!" he shouts. Then he forces the driver and everyone in the front row to the rear of the bus. He sits on the floor at the head of the aisle, his weapon across his knees.

An hour goes by. The bus is almost completely quiet. Everyone is so frightened that no one dares talk. The suspense is awful. You're sure the terrorists are in communication with government negotiators, but what's going on is anybody's guess.

You have to go to the bathroom, and it's likely others do, too. You're the nearest one to the terrorist. He's only a few feet away. He seems fairly calm now.

"Excuse me," you say. "But people have to go to the bathroom."

He glares angrily at you. Then he looks at his watch.

"Don't move!" he says. He steps outside and calls in a foreign language to the other terrorists. A moment later he comes back. "There's a toilet in the guardhouse. You can go in there," he says, pointing. "Walk in a straight line there and back or you're dead."

Turn to page 8.

The guards take you though a pair of airtight doors into a room with bare white walls and a single small, sealed window facing the hallway. There is a bed on casters, a small, straight-back steel chair, and a steel cabinet. The only other door leads to a small, windowless bathroom.

Arnoff enters, carrying a medical case. The guards make you sit in a chair. A female guard stands on one side of you, with Arnoff on the other. The woman asks you to hold out your arm. As you do so, you feel a jab in the other arm. You wheel in time to see Arnoff withdrawing a hypodermic needle.

"The virus is injected," the woman says in a toneless voice. "This room will now be sealed off. If we are correct in thinking that we have infected you with the EF1 virus, you will become highly contagious within a few hours. We will watch you through that window. There is food in the refrigerator and water in the bathroom. If you aren't very sick or dead by tomorrow morning, it will mean that what we injected you with was not the EF1 virus. Understand?"

Turn to page 103.

You recount all that happened from the moment your bus was hijacked, mentioning how you visited the cafeteria and how desperate everyone looked there. The president looks pained as he listens. You end your description by repeating Marcos's demand.

"All right," the president says with a sigh. "Thank you very much. We'll ask you to wait in the next room while we talk about this."

The minutes tick slowly by. An aide brings you the best hamburger and milk shake you have ever tasted. Or maybe it just seems that way because you're so hungry. It doesn't make you feel any less anxious, however. A staff member asks if you'd like to check a movie out of the library and watch it on the VCR, but you tell him you're too upset to watch anything. You just sit and wait another half hour until you're called.

As you walk back into the Situation Room, the president gives you a long look, his face lined with worry. "This is a very tough situation, as you are aware," he says. "You may wonder why I can't just meet their demands so we can free your classmates and your teacher. I want you to know that if I did, it would cause grave damage to the country and put many more lives in danger. The prisoners they want released include a convicted nuclear arms smuggler, an international drug czar, and a man who almost managed to blow up the Capitol. You can see what we're dealing with."

Go on to the next page.

"I sure do," you say. "It sure feels strange being in the middle of it."

"I'm sure it does," the president says gently. "I think they hope that when we see a kid standing before us, we'll think more about all the other kids on your bus, and it will be harder for us to ignore their demands. They're figuring we'll be more likely to give in. You follow me?"

"Yes, sir," you say.

"Good." He gives you a friendly smile. "Of course, the best thing would be if our special forces team—our rangers—could strike swiftly enough to save the hostages *and* destroy or capture the terrorists before they let the virus loose. And our men have an idea how that can be accomplished. We have some tactics the terrorists will never expect, but we need more time to prepare for the assault. Until then, we want Marcos to stay calm. We want to keep him talking, and we're more likely to be able to do that if we seem to be playing their game, using you as a back-and-forth mediator."

"You want me to go back there?" you say, astonished.

Turn to page 87.

"It's not true that you're holding the real vial," a voice says, "but you're still a hero." The voice belongs to Dr. Kostrikis. You hadn't seen him come into the room.

"Doctor, I'm glad you're all right," you say. "But I thought they took the real vial from you and left it on the desk. Then I switched it for a fake one."

He grins, placing an arm on your shoulder. "That was good thinking. I'd had the same idea. The one they took from me was fake—I hid the real one, and they never found it!" He shakes your hand, then steps back while Ms. Sealy gives you a hug.

A week later you see Dr. Kostrikis again. In a nationally televised ceremony, the president awards you both the Medal of Honor. The citation reads, "For your heroic and inspired action in helping foil a terrorist attack on the Biological Research Institute."

The End

"I'll tell them what you said," you say grimly. "But what shall I say about your intentions? What will you do if your demands are met?"

"You dare to ask me questions like that?" Marcos barks angrily.

At that moment the door flies open. A bushy-haired man in a white lab coat storms in. Marcos looks at him. "Yes, Arnoff?"

"We've cracked the combination," the man says. "We don't have to torch the vault."

"Good. Now leave the vial in the vault and lock it up again. It's safest right where it is."

"I want to test it. I can separate enough to try it on a patient."

"Too risky," Marcos says.

"I can do it!" Arnoff insists.

"Wait outside. I'll speak with you in a minute."

"But we shouldn't waste time!"

Marcos starts to say something, but Arnoff is already out the door. The terrorist leader returns his attention to you.

"You're thinking something," he says. "I want to know exactly what it is."

You hesitate, wondering if you should flatter him—act as if you admire him.

"Now!" Marcos shouts, snapping his fingers. "What are you thinking?"

If you decide to act as if you admire Marcos, turn to page 50.

If you decide to be straightforward, turn to page 95.

Again you're sitting before the terrorist leader. He studies you intently. "I'm sending a message to the president," he says, "but I'm not sending it with you."

You shudder, thinking that the message might *be* you—your body! But Marcos adds, "This fax machine will do just as well this time."

"What is the message?"

"That we will release the hostages, we will drop our demand that the terrorists be released from prison, and we will accept safe passage to the destination we choose."

A thrill goes through you, but you try to keep cool— you don't want to blunder now. "Good," you say. "The president does not like letting you go, but I'm sure he will be glad you're accepting his terms."

Turn to page 54.

116

Your chances of getting away with the vial seem much too slim. You lie down on your bunk, trying to think of what else to do. Soon afterward, the boat arrives, and with it the safe. You watch Marcos direct his men to lock the vial inside and realize you'll probably never get a chance to take it again.

During the months ahead you settle down to a new life. You even start going to a school, one unlike any you've attended before. In one class a woman teaches students how to make bombs. In another a man demonstrates how to plant and detect electronic bugs. In another you learn how to assemble assault weapons.

Sometimes Marcos takes you out of "school" to travel by boat, jeep, or helicopter to one of his many bases, usually for meetings with terrorists to plan attacks. It's all too clear that he's training you to be a terrorist yourself!

How can you escape? It's a question you ponder every day. Months go by, so many that you begin to despair of ever finding an answer. But your quest ends one morning when you awake in a jungle camp to the sound of helicopters overhead. *They can't be Marcos's aircraft,* you think. They're not. Seconds later a cluster of firebombs destroys the camp, along with you and everyone else in it.

The End

Scientists around the world are working frantically to find some way to combat the virus. But the odds aren't good. In fact, the situation is far graver than anyone could have imagined. The latest estimates are that unless a cure is found, the EF1 will kill a million the first month, 10 million the second month, 100 million the third month, and a billion the fourth month, and that by the end of the fifth month virtually all of humanity will be wiped out.

That's certainly not what the terrorists intended, but unless some miracle turns this thing around, that's what they're going to get.

The End

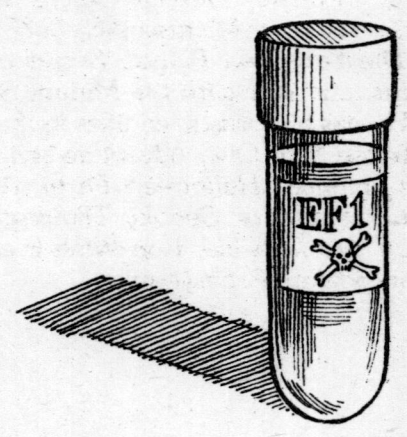

ABOUT THE AUTHOR

EDWARD PACKARD is a graduate of Princeton University and Columbia Law School. He developed the unique storytelling approach used in the Choose Your Own Adventure series while thinking up stories for his children Caroline, Andrea, and Wells.

ABOUT THE ILLUSTRATOR

RON WING is a cartoonist and illustrator who has contributed to many publications. He has illustrated many books in Bantam's Choose Your Own Adventure series, including *You Are a Millionaire, Skateboard Champion, Vampire Invaders, Outlaw Gulch, Viking Raiders, You Are Microscopic, Surf Monkeys, The Forgotten Planet, Secret of the Dolphins,* and *War with the Mutant Spider Ants.* He has also illustrated titles in the Skylark Choose Your Own Adventure series, including *Haunted Halloween Party, A Day with the Dinosaurs, Spooky Thanksgiving,* and *You Are Invisible.* Ron Wing lives and works in Benton, Pennsylvania.